"My first cat, Marshmallow, was a birth-day present from my parents when I was still little.... I waited until bedtime to tell my parents I wanted to adopt three more cats, because things are quieter then. Be-sides, I am always good about going to bed when my parents tell me. That's not one of the things I make a fuss about, but just don't try to make me eat lima beans!"

Elspeth Campbell Murphy

JULIE CHANG

Illustrated by Tony Kenyon

Chariot Books
DAVID C. COOK PUBLISHING CO.

For the Millhouse family
with love

A Wise Owl Book
Published by Chariot Books, an imprint of David C. Cook Publishing Co.
David C. Cook Publishing Co., Elgin, Illinois 60120
David C. Cook Publishing Co., Weston, Ontario

JULIE CHANG
© 1986 by Elspeth Campbell Murphy

Cover and inside illustrations by Tony Kenyon
Cover and book design by Catherine Hesz Colten

First Printing, 1986
Printed in the United States of America
90 98 88 87 86   1 2 3 4 5

Excerpt reprinted by permission of Coward-McCann, Inc. from *Millions of Cats* by Wanda Gag, copyright 1928 by Coward-McCann, Inc., copyright renewed © 1956 by Robert Janssen.

Library of Congress Cataloging-in-Publication Data

Murphy, Elspeth Campbell.
  Julie Chang.

  Summary: Although she strongly believes in the power of rules and reason, Julie discovers that good ideas don't always work and problems can't always be solved.
  [1. Conduct of life—Fiction] I. Kenyon, Tony, Ill. II. Title.
PZ7.M95316Ju   1986   [Fic]   85-27989
ISBN 0-89191-720-9

MONDAY

Dear God,

I'm writing to you in my prayer journal that Miss Jenkins gave us in Sunday school.

Mrs. Whitney, my regular school teacher, says we can have free reading and writing time when we finish our work. So I got the idea to take my prayer journal to school. And I finished my work just now, so that's why I am writing to you, God.

I guess I don't have to use my best handwriting, since this isn't going to get a grade or anything. But I think I'll do my best handwriting anyway—since it's for *you*.

I would like to use a pen, but we're not allowed to use them in school. We have to use pencils so we can erase (but I can use a pen at home). Mrs. Whitney has this poster up at school that says, "Everybody makes mistakes. That's why pencils have erasers." Miss Jenkins says the same thing—that everyone makes mistakes—and she says that you're patient with people when they mess up.

I have to stop writing pretty soon, God, because Mrs. Whitney just said she wants me to help somebody with math in a couple of minutes. Math is my best subject. Mrs. Whitney calls it buddy-study when she makes one kid help another one. But it's a funny thing. Sometimes the kid you're helping doesn't act like a buddy. Some-

6

times the person acts like you should just go away. But you can't go away, because Mrs. Whitney made you go over there in the first place. I don't know what to do when that happens.

Love,
Julie

Dear God,

This is later—at home, at night. My homework is done, and I already fed my cats, so I will write some more now. When I left off I was talking about the buddy-study at school. It worked out OK today, which was good. The person Mrs. Whitney wanted me to help was Becky Garcia. Becky is in both my regular school class and my Sunday school class, and she is a nice person. Becky *loves* to read, but she says she hates, hates, hates, hates, hates,

7

hates to do math. But today she said she doesn't mind math as much when I help her. I thought that was a nice thing to say.

My best friend, Mary Jo Bennett, is another girl who goes to regular school and Sunday school with me. Mary Jo came over to my house after school, and we did a jigsaw puzzle together.

Mary Jo is so funny the way she works on a puzzle. She just dumps all the pieces out and keeps digging through the pile. And then she tries to put the pieces in place, even if you can tell by the color that's not where they go. And she doesn't keep the piles separate, so she ends up trying the same piece over and over and over.

I kept telling her we should look for the *edge* pieces first and put them together to make a frame, and then we should gather

all the same colors together in little piles.

But when I told Mary Jo we should try doing it that way, she said, "You do it your way, and I'll do it my way." So I guess I have to let her.

I love the little snap I feel with my fingertips when a puzzle piece fits into place. And the best part of all is putting the last piece in. Mary Jo likes that part best, too. But guess what she did today, God! We were all done except for the last piece. I looked around and couldn't find it. I thought we had lost it (and I just hate, hate, hate, hate, hate, *hate* puzzles with pieces missing from them).

But then I found out that Mary Jo hid a piece in her pocket so she could be the one to put the last piece in. She figured out it didn't matter which piece she took, because whichever one she held out would be the last piece—which was good thinking, even if it was cheating.

She was going to pretend that she found the last piece on the floor, but I saw her take it out of her pocket.

I told her that what she did was cheating and that it was against the rules. Mary Jo said jigsaw puzzles don't have rules like games. But I said it still wasn't fair, and she finally agreed. But she said I still shouldn't tell her how to do puzzles.

So I made up this rule for jigsaw puzzles. Here it is: One person can't tell the other person how to work the puzzle, but no one can hide the last piece.

And then I made the rule better so it said that *both* people could keep one piece each, so there would be *two* last pieces. And then, when it was time to put those pieces in, the people had to say, "One, Two,

Three," and both put their pieces in at the same time.

So we figured that out about puzzles, and it worked out OK.

Mary Jo and I like it if my big sister, Carolyn, plays with us. Sometimes she says we are too immature to play with, but today she said OK.

She even let us look *up close* at her doll collection. My grandmother started giving these dolls to Carolyn when Carolyn was just a baby. They aren't the kind of dolls you play with. They just stand on a shelf, but if you're *very careful*, you can take them down and look at them, one at a time.

Mary Jo and I always try to decide which one of Carolyn's dolls is the prettiest. Sometimes we think we have it all figured out, but then we change our minds.

12

This afternoon Mary Jo and I decided that we liked the Chinese doll the best because of her long, black hair and her silk dress that just kind of floats around her. Her name is Lihwa, and you say it like this: LEE-hwah.

My grandmother helped Carolyn pick out the name. Grandmother says that long ago there was a beautiful Chinese princess who had that name, Lihwa, and—guess what! Her other name was Chang, just like us! Isn't that nice? Lihwa, the princess, had long hair. You know *how* long? Seven feet!! When my grandmother first told us that, Carolyn and I got out a ruler and string and cut the string to be seven feet long. And then I tied the string on my head and pretended it was my real hair.

I have long hair, but not that long. Sometime I will write about why I have long hair, God.

My little sister Amy, who is in kindergarten, saw that Carolyn was letting us take the dolls down, so she came right over. And when Amy heard Mary Jo and me picking Lihwa as the prettiest doll, she said Lihwa was her favorite, too. But we couldn't tell whether she really thinks that or whether she was just copying us. You know kindergartners.

14

Amy leaves her own dolls all over the house, and sometimes their hair is pulled out and they don't even have all their clothes on. And then Amy wants to play with Carolyn's dolls. But, of course, Carolyn says NO WAY. (I don't blame her, do you, God?)

Love,
Julie

TUESDAY

Dear God,

I just got this good idea. Do you want to hear what it is? Well, the thing I like to write most is reports. I write them for real school and when we play school, too. And now I just got the idea that I can write reports in my prayer journal. No one else will read them—just you. I think you will like them, because Miss Jenkins says you're always interested in everything that happens to people.

So here is my first report, God.

My Big Sister, Carolyn, and My Little Sister, Amy
by Julie Chang

Carolyn is in the sixth grade, and mostly she is interested in music. She plays the piano and takes lessons twice a week and practices every day without being yelled at to do it. In fact, my parents try to get her to do other things *besides* play the piano. Her teacher says she is the best pupil he ever had and that Carolyn could be a very famous piano player someday.

So Carolyn always has music on her mind. I usually have a lot of different things on my mind—like saving up money to buy toys for my cats (I will tell you about them in another report, God) and whose turn it is to feed the gerbils at school and where everybody will probably sit when Mrs. Whitney moves our desks.

17

Then there is Amy. I don't think Amy has *anything* on her mind. Everybody who knows her says that she is a little clown.

One time we saw these otters at the zoo. They were sliding down their little hill and splashing into the water and chasing each other and just having fun. And I said to my family, "They remind me of Amy," and everybody laughed, even Carolyn, because the otters *did* act just like Amy.

Amy is fun, but she can drive a person crazy. She *really* drives Carolyn crazy, because Carolyn likes to have everything JUST SO, and Amy is pretty sloppy.

So now I have told you about Carolyn and Amy, my two sisters. I think it is good that people don't all have to be one way for you to love them, God. I think it is good that you love Carolyn, who is always neat and serious. And I think it is good that you love Amy, who is sloppy and silly.

And I think it is *really good* that you love me, who is sort of in the middle.

WEDNESDAY

Why My House Has the Rooms It Does
by Julie Chang

Now I will tell you about our house, God, even though you already know what it looks like. Pastor Bennett at Apple Street Church, who is my friend Mary Jo's father, says you can see us and be with us no matter where we are. I think that's good. My mother says she sometimes wishes *she* could be two places at the same time so she could get more stuff done, but I never heard of any people who could do that.

Anyway, our house has three downstairs

bedrooms, but that's not how all those rooms are used.

It's like this: My parents have one bedroom. And my father made one of the littler bedrooms into his office. (He has a regular job, but he has another at-home job where he helps people with their taxes and stuff.)

And my mother made the other little bedroom into a sewing office, because she is really a good *seamstress,* which is the special word for a lady who sews. People pay her to make things for them. (But she is mostly a mother.)

Anyway, Carolyn, Amy, and I all share a room upstairs. It is a big attic room, almost as big as the whole house, I think.

My father says he is going to put up dividers so that it will be like three medium-sized rooms, one for each of us kids.

But until that happens, we just have to pretend that the dividers are there. Carolyn pretends the most of all.

She has this imaginary wall and this imaginary door. And Amy and I can't come in Carolyn's part of the room unless we knock first.

But the trouble is, there's no door to knock on, so we have to knock on the floor or walk over to the nearest wall and knock.

I made up this rule for our room that says we can't get into each other's stuff. (Carolyn says especially not her doll collection.)

The rule I made up says if we want to borrow something, we have to ask. And if the person says, "No," we can ask one more time. But if the person still says, "No," we have to stop asking, because then it's *pes-*

tering. (And if the person says, "No," we're not allowed to take the stuff just because we asked, either.)

I printed that rule in my best printing and used my felt-tipped markers, which I like to keep nice. Then I taped the rule on the door where we could all see it—especially Amy. Because—so what if she can't read? She knows the sign means business.

I made a copy of the rules for my mother, because she likes to keep up with what's going on. She said "thank you" very nicely and hung the rules up in her sewing office.

SATURDAY

Dear God,

It is a cold, rainy Saturday afternoon. Carolyn is over at a friend's house, and Amy is over in Carolyn's part of the room, looking up at the doll collection. Wait a minute, OK? I'd better go get her.

I'm back. I told Amy to get away from Carolyn's stuff, and Amy said, "Lihwa's hair is messy. I'd better comb it."

And I said, "Lihwa's hair is not the least bit messy. And if you try to comb it, you'll just ruin it." But I knew how Amy felt. I would just love to pull the ribbons out of

Lihwa's hair and then comb it and braid it again.

You know what, God? Sometimes the rule about not getting into other people's stuff is a hard one to follow.

But I still have to keep Amy out of trouble, so maybe I will read to her.

Love,
Julie

Dear God,

This is still Saturday but it is later, and Amy is downstairs, talking my mother into making popcorn.

I just got done reading to Amy. And it did keep her mind off Carolyn's stuff. For a while, anyway.

Amy's favorite book is called *Millions of Cats*. It's nice that book is Amy's favorite, because I picked it out specially as her

25

birthday present from Carolyn and me. (I think it's nice when you buy somebody a present and it turns out to be their favorite thing, don't you?)

But, of course, Amy loves just about any kind of present. And she *really loves* BIRTHDAYS! Some other day I will write about how *much* Amy loves birthdays, God. Then you'll know what I'm talking about, believe me.

Anyway, when I was reading out loud, Amy wasn't the only one listening to the story. One of my cats, Sumi, always comes from wherever she is in the house as soon as she hears me start reading to Amy. She comes and sits right down next to Amy to listen to the story. It makes me feel like a teacher with a strange class—one little girl and a cat.

Sumi does this all the time. At first I

wondered if she somehow knew that *Millions of Cats* was about cats. But one day, just to find out, I read Amy a book called *Curious George,* which is about a monkey. And sure enough, Sumi came for that story, too. It's the same no matter what story I read.

I asked Mrs. Whitney, my regular school teacher, about why Sumi does that. She said maybe Sumi likes the sound of my voice when I'm reading and that Sumi can tell the difference between when I'm reading and just talking. I think that's true. I love it when Mrs. Whitney reads to us in school. And I love it when Pastor Bennett reads the Bible in church. I don't always understand what all the Bible words mean, but I like the sound of them, anyway.

Amy's favorite part of *Millions of Cats* is when it says,
   "Cats here, cats there,
   Cats and kittens everywhere,
   Hundreds of cats,
   Thousands of cats,
   Millions and billions and trillions of
      cats."
I love cats SO MUCH that I would love to have millions of them, too, God. But in the story, the very old man and the very old woman ended up with just one cat. So I will be glad I have my five cats.

One time we had to write reports at school about our pets, so I wrote about my cats—all five of them. Danny Petrowski, who is good at drawing, made pictures for the bulletin board, and Mrs. Whitney picked some of our reports to put on the board for display. One kid, whose report didn't get picked, asked me if Mrs. Whitney picked mine just because it was so long.

I felt sorry for her that her report didn't get picked. I don't know if the reason was that it was too short or what. But she acted like she thought I was showing off by having a long report. I tried to tell her my report *had* to be long, because I have five cats. But then it sounded like I was bragging about having so many pets.

I think sometimes people think you're snotty when you're not—it's just that you can't think of the right, nice thing to say. So both of you just sit there, and both of you feel bad. I wish no one ever had to feel bad, God. Why do they?

Love,
Julie

SUNDAY

How I Got My Five Cats
by Julie Chang

You know, God, when people find out that there are *five cats* at my house, they can't believe it, because that is quite a few cats. But *then,* when people find out the cats are MOSTLY MINE and not just my family's, they are *really* surprised. They say, "Wow! Are you lucky! How come your parents let you have *five cats*?"

If there's not enough time, I just tell people, "It's a long story." But if there *is* time, then I tell them the whole thing.

Mary Jo likes the story about my cat

called Oreo best, and she always wants me to skip ahead to that one and tell it first. But I think you should start at the beginning and tell something that way.

Well, anyway, God, you know how it happened. Miss Jenkins says you understand everything. I wish I understood everything. I hate it when something doesn't make any sense.

Anyway, when people ask me about my cats, I tell them what happened.

I tell them I didn't get all the cats at once. I mean, I didn't just walk into a pet store and tell my father I wanted five kittens, because then I don't think he would have said OK. The way it happened, he didn't have to say a big OK all at once. He just had to say a little OK a few times.

Marshmallow (Cat Number One)
by Julie Chang

My first cat was a birthday present from my parents when I was still little, I think in the first grade.

I had been asking for a cat for a long time. In fact, my mother says when I was just a baby, I used to bounce up and down in my stroller whenever I saw a cat and yell, "Mine kitty! Mine kitty!" Little kids think everything they want is theirs, I guess.

Anyway, my first cat's name is Marshmallow, and as people can tell from the name, he is all white. Marshmallow is the *sweetest, cutest, cuddliest,* most *adorable* cat in the whole world. He *loves* attention. In fact, he'll take all the attention he can get.

One time Mary Jo tried to trade her

snotty cat, old Mr. Ferguson, for Marshmallow. But I said NO WAY!!!!!

Mr. Ferguson won't even play with a person who *likes* cats. Now I can understand if he wants to ignore people who don't like him, but when a person *likes* cats, I think it would be a good rule for the cat to like that person back. I guess you couldn't really make a rule that all cats would obey—especially not Mr. Ferguson. He would only ignore the rule, because that's just the way he is.

So Marshmallow is my first cat, and he will always be my special favorite. But I try to keep that a secret from the other cats.

MONDAY

Dear God,

For some reason I got up extra early this morning, so I will have some time to write to you. Also, I will have even more extra time. Know why? Because this is my morning to walk Amy to school, and she's always running around at the last minute.

Carolyn and I have to take turns getting Amy to school and back because of something Amy did this summer just before school started. *Wait till you hear about it!*

Our school has an all-day kindergarten now, and Amy goes to that. When I was little, I just went half a day. I don't think

35

kindergartners are any smarter now than they used to be, do you? Just look at Amy.

Sometimes Carolyn takes her in the morning, and I pick her up in the afternoon. And sometimes it's the other way around.

Anyway, I was going to tell you what Amy did. Of course, you know how much Amy *loves* BIRTHDAYS! Well . . .

It was in the summer just before school started, and Amy went out of our backyard, which she's not supposed to do without asking my mother's permission. Nobody saw where she went, but then my mother noticed she was gone. And that's when my mother just went wild. She kept yelling, "Where's Amy? Where's Amy? So everybody had to go looking for her. Carolyn and her piano teacher and Mary Jo and me and the neighbors and everyone.

Mary Jo and I were hunting up and down the alley, and we came to this house that had a little kid's birthday party going on in the backyard. Mary Jo got all excited because they had pony rides at the party, and Mary Jo is *crazy* about horses. But then I looked at the pony, and who do you think was riding it? AMY!

Amy didn't even know the kid whose birthday it was, but she likes birthdays so much, she just walked in the yard and joined the party! And there were so many kids running around that the mother didn't even notice the extra one, and not even the birthday kid noticed that Amy didn't bring a present. So Amy had a good time. She had cake and ice cream. She got to ride a pony. She even won a couple of prizes!

As soon as we found her, Mary Jo and I

grabbed her and practically carried her home. And then, when my mother saw Amy safe and sound, she went even wilder and started hugging Amy and spanking her all at the same time.

When my father got home, my mother wanted him to yell at Amy some more. He was really mad that Amy just walked off the way she did, but every time he thought about her going to the birthday party of someone she didn't even know, he started laughing—and he doesn't usually laugh right out loud that much. But of course he wanted Amy to know how bad she had been. So he went into another room to try and get all laughed out and come back serious. But as soon as he saw Amy he just started laughing again.

This happened *three times,* and each time Carolyn and I were laughing so hard we couldn't sit up, and tears were running down our faces and we couldn't stop them.

Finally my mother said, "I don't think it will do any good to talk to Amy anymore." Then she said we would *all* have to watch Amy like a hawk.

That birthday party happened in the summer, and now the weather is getting colder, but my mother *still* makes Carolyn and me watch Amy like a hawk. Probably when I am 109 and Amy is 105, I will still have to watch her like a hawk and walk her everywhere.

Amy is *finally* ready for school, so I have to go now. Today I will have to *run* her to school, so we won't be late.

Love,
Julie

Dear God,

Today something really nice happened, and it was quite a surprise. Sometimes I think it would be good always to know what's going to happen. But then I think, you wouldn't get any surprises that way. And sometimes the best things just happen, and you didn't *make* them happen. They're just there.

Here's what I'm talking about:

This afternoon Carolyn came home from being at the shopping mall with her friends. They all came upstairs to our attic room, and Carolyn walked over kind of matter-of-factly and dropped this tiny, blue paper bag into my hands.

"What's this?" I asked.

"Open it," she said.

"Is it for me?" I asked.

"No," she said. "It's for the man in the moon. Of course it's for you."

So I opened the little bag, and inside there was a little cardboard square with four barrettes pinned on it. And on each barrette was a little Siamese cat.

I think I made a funny little gasping noise, because Carolyn and her friends laughed. But the barrettes were *so neat!*

And Carolyn bought them for me with her own money in front of her friends and *gave* them to me in front of her friends.

Carolyn said, "I thought of you when I saw them, because you have Siamese cats and long hair. I know you have three Siamese cats but they only had cards with four barrettes."

I said, "That's OK! I can wear one for each cat and keep the extra barrette for a spare. Thank you, Carolyn! I love them!"

"Yeah, OK," said Carolyn. "Where's Amy? I figured I'd better get her something, too."

The thing Carolyn got for Amy was popcorn from one of those special stores that sell nothing but popcorn in all different flavors and colors. Amy's favorite popcorn is pink. She doesn't like the taste, but she thinks it looks beautiful. So Carolyn remembered that and got some for her.

When Carolyn and her friends were gone, I carefully took the barrettes off the card and put them on my bedspread. First I put them in a square, and then I made them go out like sunbeams. And on and on like that. Then I put the extra barrette back on the card and put it in my drawer where I could keep it for a spare and not lose it.

The three little Siamese barrette-cats reminded me of the cat report I am working on for you, God. I will work on it again, soon, but now I want to show my mother what Carolyn got me.

Love,
Julie

Dear God,

This is later, and I am wearing the barrettes now—I couldn't wait for tomorrow morning. Before I do the next part of my cat report, I thought of another little report I could write.

Why I Have Long Hair
by Julie Chang

Mornings are my favorite time, because that's when my mother does my hair. She says long hair looks pretty, but that you have to take care of it.

Carolyn and Amy both wanted short hair, because they are too busy for long hair.

But in the morning I pick out the ribbons or barrettes I want to wear, and I tell my mother how I want my hair to look that day. And she fixes it. I don't yell even when she accidentally pulls too hard. It's a good time to be alone with my mother. Sometimes we talk, and sometimes we don't. And either way it's all right.

Just now I asked my mother if Princess Lihwa's mother did Lihwa's hair. But my mother said Lihwa probably had servants back then to do her seven-foot-long hair.

I think having your mother do your hair is nicer than if servants do it.

TUESDAY

Lady Suki, Lady Sumi, and Lady Setsu (Cat Number Two, Cat Number Three, and Cat Number Four)
by Julie Chang

After Marshmallow, here's how I got the next three cats, God. It was different from the way I got Marshmallow, because these three came all together—and they weren't kittens and they belonged to somebody else. So, in a way, they're not exactly mine—not the way Marshmallow is.

Remember the nice old lady, Mrs. Riley, who used to live down the street from me, God? She used to live next door to Danny

Petrowski, the kid in my Sunday school class and regular school class who draws so well.

Anyway, Mrs. Riley and I were good friends, even though she was an old lady and I was a kid. That's because we both like cats so much. I used to take Marshmallow over to visit her and her three Siamese cats named Lady Suki, Lady Sumi, and Lady Setsu, which are Japanese names. (Just like Carolyn's doll Lihwa has a Chinese name.)

Then it got so Mrs. Riley was sick a lot of the time and couldn't take care of herself, so she had to move into a nursing home.

And the thing was—the nursing home didn't allow pets. She worried about getting a good home for them where they could all stay together. You see, she didn't want them to miss her and their house and each other all at the same time.

And she kept saying, "What's going to happen to my cats?" I think she was more worried about them than she was about herself being sick.

And that's when I got my good idea. The thing about good ideas that you have to watch out for is this, God: you have to keep quiet until the time is right to tell someone your idea. Otherwise, you could ruin everything.

I got the idea to *adopt* Lady Suki, Lady Sumi, and Lady Setsu and take them to live at my house!!! That way they would be together and they could live in their old neighborhood and be with someone they knew (me) who would love them and take care of them. And I could send Mrs. Riley pictures of them and write her reports about how they were getting along so she wouldn't worry so much.

I wanted to tell Mrs. Riley right away because I was so excited, but I stopped myself—because I had to ask my parents first. If I told her, and then my parents said NO WAY, I would have to take my idea back, and that would be really embarrassing.

So I waited until bedtime to tell my parents, because things are quieter then. My father says he always likes to sleep on a problem. And no matter how much you pester him, you can't get him to decide about something—especially if it's important—until the next day. Besides, I am always good about going to bed when my parents tell me. Some kids I know make a lot of fuss so they can stay up later. That's not one of the things I make a fuss about, but just don't try to make me eat lima beans! So I thought I should ask my parents about my good idea when they could see me being a really nice kid.

I reminded them about Mrs. Riley and the nursing home. And then I reminded them about how I always took care of Marshmallow without having to be told to. I said if I could take such good care of *one* cat, I could take care of *four*.

My father thinks about money a lot, and he said it would take *lots of money* to feed all those cats. But I said Mrs. Riley didn't know what to do. Then my mother got little tears in the corner of her eyes, and my father said he would have to sleep on the problem and that I would just have to wait. But I knew that was coming, so it was OK.

The next morning at breakfast my parents said I could have Mrs. Riley's cats, because Christians should help each other and it would be a load off Mrs. Riley's mind to know her cats had a good home.

But they told me the *good home* was my responsibility. If I had four cats, I had to take *good care* of them.

And that's the way it still is, God. Even with *five* cats, which I have now. (Reminder: Report on Cat Number Five will be coming up later.)

Every day I have to feed them (even though, if you want to know the truth, God, I don't like the smell of cat food too much). And I have to change their drinking water. (I've gotten so I can do that without spilling a drop.)

My mother helps me with the kitty litter. But I have to keep track of when we need more kitty litter and cat food and write down how much to buy on the shopping list. It's a lot of responsibility.

When Carolyn heard that Lady Suki, Lady Sumi, and Lady Setsu were coming to live at our house, she said, "You'd better keep those cats off my bed. And they'd better not go walking on the shelves and knock over my doll collection."

But it turned out the new cats didn't bother Carolyn. They bothered Amy instead. You'll never guess what happened. They thought Amy's doll furniture was just right for them!

Lady Suki took over the doll buggy. Lady Sumi took over the doll chair. And Lady Setsu took over the doll bed. And no matter how much Amy cried and tried to push them off, *nothing* could make them give up that furniture.

So finally my father got some new doll furniture for Amy. And he said these cats were costing him money.

We moved the old doll furniture to my part of the attic room, and everything is calm now.

But it wasn't always calm.

At first The Ladies kept running away to their old house, because that was where they thought they belonged—and they would meow to get in. So then the new people would call me up and I would go get the cats. I would go next door to get Danny to help me. And he would say, "Don't tell me. Let me guess. It's those cats again." Usually Pug McConnell would be over at Danny's, so they would both help me take the cats home.

The Ladies don't run away anymore, so I guess they are used to me.

54

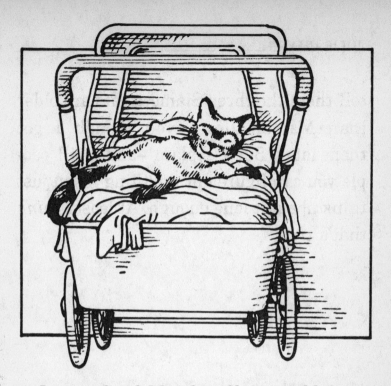

I was afraid Marshmallow wouldn't get used to having three more cats around, and he didn't like it at first. But Suki, Sumi, and Setsu kind of stay by themselves. They are a lot older than Marshmallow, and I think they look down on him and don't like to play with him because they think he's immature.

Sometimes people get confused when I

tell them the three Siamese cats are older than Marshmallow—even though I got them later. But I explain—and I tell people you can figure out anything if you just think about it long enough. At least I *think* that's true.

WEDNESDAY

Dear God,

Today Mary Jo Bennett, Becky Garcia, and I went to the public library together.

Mary Jo and I couldn't believe Becky! Usually Becky is so quiet in school she hardly makes a peep, but the librarian is her special friend and they talked a lot about the books Becky just brought back. Becky could remember all about who was in the books and what happened and everything.

Then we went to get more books, and when we brought them up to the checkout desk, I said you could tell whose books were whose just by reading the titles. Mary Jo checked out all horse stories, including one book she's already read four times. I checked out cat books, and Becky checked out everything else. She had a couple of mysteries and a book of fairy tales and even a biography of Clara Barton (Becky told us Clara Barton was an old-time nurse) and a book of poetry. When Mary Jo saw Becky's poetry book, she went charging back to get one, too, and knocked over a plant on the way. (But it turned out to be plastic, so there wasn't a big mess.)

Mary Jo likes poems, but she never remembers you can get poetry books at the library, too.

On the way home, Mary Jo told me to tell Becky about how I got my cat Oreo. So

I did. And while I'm thinking of Oreo, I can finish my cat report.

Love,
Julie

Oreo (Cat Number Five)
by Julie Chang

If people *still* have enough time after I tell them about Cats One through Four, God, I tell them about how I got Oreo.

Oreo is a sweet, sweet little kitten. I named him Oreo, because he is black on one end and white in the middle and black on the other end. He reminded me of an Oreo cookie, so that's why I called him Oreo.

People probably think the last thing in the world I needed was another cat, but Oreo was this poor, little, lost kitten who was hanging around in the alley. He didn't belong to anyone—because I checked. I asked at all the houses, but no one knew where he came from. So I thought I would ask my parents if I could keep him.

But I thought that was kind of pushing my luck, because how many parents let their kids have even four cats? But Oreo was so cute, I thought maybe if they accidently saw him in our yard they would just make up their own minds to keep him without me having to ask.

But Oreo was so shy, I didn't know how to get him into my yard. And if I took my parents to the little hole where Oreo slept, they would know something was up for sure.

I didn't want just to grab Oreo, because that would scare him. So I pretended I accidently dropped some cat food outside

of his little hole. (It was really on purpose.) And I dropped some more right up the alley. Then I kind of left the gate open and put more food in our yard. And sure enough, Oreo came right into our yard!

I still didn't grab Oreo, but I closed the gate behind him so he couldn't run away. It was time for supper then, and, sure enough, my father looked out the window and said, "What's that cat doing in our yard?"

I kept very calm, which was good—but then I made a mistake. I said, "Oh, it's just Oreo." And my father looked at me very hard and said very slowly, "How do you know his name is Oreo? Do you know that cat? Did you put him in our yard?"

So I started explaining about how he had nowhere to live except a little hole in the ground. And how I had named him

Oreo because he probably didn't even have a name and even if he did it couldn't be better than Oreo. And how he was just a poor, little, motherless kitten.

And my mother started getting tears in the corners of her eyes. And then Carolyn said kind of matter-of-factly, "It's starting to rain."

And *then* (this is Mary Jo's favorite part of the story, God) my mother and I jumped up at exactly the same time and ran outside and picked Oreo up very quickly (but gently) and brought him into the house.

Oreo was mewing, and my mother and I were crying. And Amy started crying just because we were.

My father rubbed his eyes with both hands the way he does when people don't keep all their receipts and said, "This is absolutely, positively the *Last Cat!*"

It took me a minute to realize that he was saying I could KEEP Oreo. And then I just started crying more, because I was so happy.

Marshmallow was more jealous of Oreo than he was of Mrs. Riley's cats. So I had to keep Marshmallow and Oreo in separate rooms for a while and let them get to know each other a little bit at a time.

I told Mary Jo to come over and act like Oreo was *her* cat until Marshmallow got used to having Oreo living here. So now everything is calm and OK. I can get worn out cuddling them all sometimes, but I don't mind.

So, God, that's my report on how I got my five cats. And I really don't think I'm going to get any more.

THURSDAY

Dear God,

I had a nice day at school today. It was one of those days where if someone asked, "What made it so nice?" I wouldn't know how to answer. It was just—nice. I love days like that when everything is fine.

Love,
Julie

FRIDAY

Dear God,

I'm going to take my prayer journal to school with me again today. That way, if I have any extra time, I can write to you.

Love,
Julie

8:30 a.m.

Dear God,

It's still early, but two big things happened already! The first was really big, and the second was kind of big.

First of all, I was walking to school with Mary Jo and Amy this morning, and I

66

couldn't believe what that kid did—Amy, I mean.

The thing you have to understand about Amy is that she doesn't like to wear jackets, mittens, scarves, or hats. She would just rather freeze.

It's getting cold these days, so Mother bundles Amy up. But then *I* have the job of making sure Amy keeps her coat on.

Today, instead of wearing her scarf, Amy was carrying it, and the way she had it bundled up looked kind of funny.

So I said sternly, "Amy Louise, you put that scarf on right this minute!"

But Amy said, "No!" And then she hugged the scarf closer.

That made me suspicious. And I said even sterner, "Amy Louise, do you have something wrapped up in that scarf? You let me see right now."

67

Of course, Amy said, "No!" She looked kind of stubborn and scared at the same time. That's how she always looks when she's up to something.

And was she ever up to something!

I took the scarf away from her and unwrapped it. I couldn't believe my eyes. Amy had taken Carolyn's beautiful Chinese doll, Lihwa.

Mary Jo said, "Amy, what in the world are you doing with Carolyn's doll?"

It turned out Amy was taking it for kindergarten Show and Tell.

I said, "Amy, Carolyn didn't say you could borrow her doll, did she?"

Amy just shook her head.

Then I said, "You didn't even ask her, did you?"

Amy just shook her head again. We both knew it wouldn't do any good to ask, be-

cause Carolyn wouldn't say "yes" in millions and billions and trillions of years.

Then I said, "Amy! You *know* the rule we have about not messing with each other's stuff! Why did I go to all the trouble of making up that good rule if you're not going to obey it? I even printed a sign. So what if you can't read? You know the sign means business!"

So I told Amy to give Lihwa to me and I would take care of her for the day because it was too late to take her home.

Amy didn't like the idea, but she knows when she's licked. I told her, "Now here's the plan. I'll take care of the doll, because she will be safer with me, because I'm older. When Carolyn comes to get you after school, you walk *as slow as you can*. I'll run home and put the doll back before Carolyn finds out you took her. OK?"

Amy nodded like she understood, but you never know with kindergartners.

So Mary Jo and I dropped Amy off and went to our own room.

Mary Jo asked me what I was going to do with Lihwa, and I said I thought my desk would be the best place—that way I could keep an eye on her.

I thought about showing the doll to the class when Mrs. Whitney has "Sharing Our Experiences," but then I figured it wouldn't be fair for me to use Carolyn's doll for my own Show and Tell when I wouldn't let Amy do that.

And that's when the *second* big thing happened, God.

When we came up to the coat rack outside our room, we could hear the kids saying, "A sub! A sub!" They were already trying to figure out if she would be mean

71

or nice and how much they could act up.

Miss MacDonald, the substitute, is still trying to get things organized, and that's why I have time to write all this. (She said we could have Study Time to finish our homework, and mine is already finished.)

Mrs. Whitney changed everybody's seat again last week, so now Mary Jo and I sit right next to each other, which is nice.

I tucked Lihwa inside my sweater to get her into the room, and now she's safe in my desk. I didn't want to show her to anyone, because I didn't feel like people asking me a lot of questions about her.

Besides, I didn't know if the sub would take the doll away if she saw it.

Some teachers just take toys away first thing, because they figure you're going to play with them sooner or later, even if you say you're not.

I think Miss MacDonald is reading a note Mrs. Whitney left.

Mrs. Whitney has this rule that says whenever she's gone Curtis Anderson and I are supposed to be T.A.s for the day, because Mrs. Whitney says we're dependable.

T.A. stands for "Teacher's Assistant." The sub is supposed to pick Curtis for the boy T.A. and me for the girl T.A. So I hope Miss MacDonald knows she's supposed to do that. Probably Mrs. Whitney told her in the note.

The other part of the regular T. A. rule is that the T. A. can always pick a friend to be the T. A.'s helper. So of course I will pick Mary Jo, because she and I have our own rule that we will pick each other.

Love,
Julie

9:00 a.m.
Dear God,

When I was on my way up to the teacher's desk just now to get my T.A. badge, I heard someone whisper, "That dumb Julie always thinks she's so special."

I looked around, but I couldn't figure out who said it.

It really hurt my feelings, God! Because, that's not the way I am at all. I don't think I act like I'm better than everybody else. I really try to be nice to everybody and not be snotty. I mean, I think it should work out that if you're a nice person, people shouldn't talk about you and say you're snotty when you're not.

Mrs. Whitney always says we should just forget it when someone says something mean, but I don't know how to do that. I think if someone—even if you don't

74

know who—hurts your feelings first thing in the morning, it can make the whole day seem bad.

It can even ruin being T.A. if people think you're a snotty T.A. when you're not.

Love,
Julie

9:35 a.m.
Dear God,

I finished my math assignment early. Usually when we have a sub we just do practice work and not new stuff. And math is the thing I do fastest anyway.

The kids aren't being very good for Miss MacDonald. She has this funny thing she does where she says everything twice. Like, she doesn't just say, "Be quiet, and get out your math books." She says, "All right. All right. Be quiet. Quiet. Now get

75

out your math books. Your math books."

Most of the kids haven't noticed she does that, but a couple of the kids are starting to say everything twice, too. Like, "Miss MacDonald. Miss MacDonald. May I sharpen my pencil? My pencil?"

I hate it when things go wrong. You know, like when kids act up for the sub. I feel like I should do something about it, since I'm supposed to be a dependable T.A. But I don't know what to do.

Miss MacDonald finally said that if she has one more problem with this class, she will leave Mrs. Whitney a note.

Mrs. Whitney left a note for the sub that says if we're bad, she'll take away the puppet show when she comes back on Monday. Everyone else in the school will get to go except our class.

So the kids got pretty quiet after that.

But they're still not as good as when Mrs. Whitney is here. I wish Mrs. Whitney were here today. I just like it better when things are the way they're supposed to be.

We're not supposed to talk, so Mary Jo wrote me a note and asked if Carolyn's doll was OK. I peeked in my desk, and the doll is fine. I'm just nervous about the whole thing though. I wish Amy hadn't taken Lihwa. I wish Lihwa were back on the shelf in Carolyn's part of the attic room where she belongs.

Love,
Julie

11:10 a.m.
Dear God,

It's almost time for lunch now.

At recess I asked Mary Jo what happened to the note she wrote me about the doll, because I thought Miss MacDonald might not like it if we were passing notes—even though we were done with our work and not making any noise.

Mary Jo said the note must have dropped on the floor. We looked around for it, but we couldn't find it.

The kids are not lining up neatly in ABC order the way we're supposed to when we go to lunch. We have to be careful or we'll lose the puppet show, because when Mrs. Whitney says something, she means it.

It's all kind of disorganized today. I have to go now. Sometimes I wish I could trade places with Marshmallow or Oreo and just be cozy at home.

Love,
Julie

12:20 p.m.

Dear God,

I'm back from lunch now, and the most terrible thing has happened!

Lihwa is gone! I checked my desk as soon as I came in from the lunchroom, and Carolyn's beautiful doll is gone!

I left the doll in my desk at lunch, because I thought she would be safer there. I didn't want to get something spilled on her or have people asking to play with her and comb her hair.

I thought I did the right thing, God, but Lihwa is still gone, and I don't know what to do! I feel like I'm going to start to cry, and then everyone will think that I'm not a good T.A.

Miss MacDonald said we could have free reading and writing time at our desks as long as we're quiet, and she reminded us about the puppet show. She's meaner now than she was this morning.

Mary Jo figured notes would be OK since it's free reading and writing time, so here are the notes she wrote me and that I wrote back to her.

Julie, what's wrong? You look like you're going to cry or something.

Carolyn's doll is gone. Lihwa's not in my desk.

Where is she?

I don't know. She's gone. Somebody took her.

Who?

I don't know.

Maybe you should tell Miss MacDonald.

I guess so. But if I tell her, Miss Mac-Donald will get mad that the whole thing happened, and she'll probably take away the puppet show. Then everybody will be mad at *me*. And they'll look at me with really snotty looks and say, "Thanks a lot, Julie."

Maybe we can find out who took Lihwa and get her back ourselves.

How? Miss MacDonald isn't letting people get out of their seats.

I know. But you're the T.A., and I'm the T.A.'s friend. If she tells us to pass out papers or something, we can kind of look in people's desks as we go by.

That's a good idea. Probably a girl took the doll. Should we look in the boys' desks, too, or just the girls'?

A boy might have taken the doll to give to his sister.

Maybe, but let's mostly check the girls' desks.

82

OK. And we don't have to check Becky's, because she's not here today.

Unless somebody hid the doll in her desk.

That could be.

So we'll just check the best we can, right?

Right.

1:30 p.m.
Dear God,
Well, that was a really good idea that Mary Jo and I had, except it didn't work. I don't understand that. I don't know why ideas don't always work out—especially when they're good ones.

Miss MacDonald did tell Mary Jo and me to pass out papers, and we were really excited, because we thought we had our chance. We peeked in the desks as we went by, but not all the girls had their desks open, and some of them looked at us funny—like they knew something was up. So our good idea didn't work. I thought my problem was going to be over, but now I feel worse than ever. I don't like it when things get this messed up.

It started to drizzle some a little while ago, so we're having indoor recess now. Miss MacDonald said we don't have to play 7-Up if we don't want to, but we have to be quiet so the players can concentrate.

Mary Jo wrote me some more notes instead of playing, and I wrote back to her.

Julie, the doll might still be in some-

84

body's desk. But maybe she's somewhere else. I wish we could get up and hunt for her. It makes me itchy just to sit here.

I know, but the only ones allowed out of their seats are the people who are tapping other people's thumbs.

If we get up, Miss MacDonald will yell at us.

Maybe we can figure out where Lihwa is just by looking. She's about the size of a ruler. Where could you hide something kind of long and skinny?

In a lunch box?

No, because a lunch box wouldn't be long enough. The doll would be too big.

Not if you broke the doll in half.

Mary Jo!! Don't even *think* that! Anyway, why would the person who stole the doll do that? If you're going to steal a doll, you don't want a broken one.

I guess you're right. A book bag?

That might work if a person didn't have a lot of papers and stuff in it already. She'd have to take some stuff out, probably, to make room for the doll.

Julie, I've got it! I bet the doll is rolled up in the map over the blackboard.

That would be a good hiding place, all right, but how did the person get up that high?

86

Climbed up. You could put a chair on a desk. And if that didn't work, you could put a chair on a chair on a desk.

Maybe.

How about in the cabinets under the sink?

Kids aren't supposed to open those cabinets.

I know. But if a person is mean enough to steal another person's sister's doll, she probably doesn't care about the sink rule.

Mary Jo, do you think I am nice to everybody?

I think you're very nice.

Then why would someone do this mean thing to me?

I don't know.

Well, what am I going to do? Carolyn will never talk to me again. And she'll think she shouldn't have bothered to buy me Siamese cat barrettes, because I don't deserve them. All I did was try to keep Amy out of trouble, and now look what happened!

Don't worry. You'll think of something. You always have something up your sleeve.

Not today I don't. This is the worst day I ever had. MARY JO! THAT'S IT!

What's it?

A sleeve! Someone could have put Lihwa up the sleeve of a jacket. The doll is kind of long and skinny, and so is a sleeve. That would be the *perfect* place to hide her.

But the doll would fall out.

Not if you stuck a mitten or scarf in the end, she wouldn't. If I could get out to the coat rack, all I would have to do is squeeze the sleeves on the jackets, and I could tell if the doll was in there. MARY JO, STOP BOUNCING UP AND DOWN, OR MISS MACDONALD WILL YELL AT YOU AND TAKE AWAY THE PUPPET SHOW.

I can't help it! I'm so excited about your idea! How are you going to get out to the coat rack to find out? I know! You could

89

ask Miss MacDonald if you could use the bathroom.

But I don't need to go.

That doesn't matter. You could just tell her that as a reason to leave the room.

But isn't that like telling a lie?

I don't know.

I think it is. Maybe Miss MacDonald will give me a note to take somewhere.

2:30 p.m.
Dear God,
Well, I guess you know that's how it happened, God. Miss MacDonald sent me with a note to the office that said she need-

ed someone to bring a movie projector to the classroom so she could show us this movie about tractors.

The T.A. always gets to take notes to the office, but I'm just glad Miss MacDonald asked me instead of Curtis.

On the way back I stopped and tried out my idea. I was so excited and nervous. I was afraid Miss MacDonald would wonder what was taking me so long.

I squeezed the arms on all the jackets. I could hardly believe it when my idea was *right* and I felt the doll inside one of the sleeves. Right away I looked to see whose jacket it was.

It was Mary Jo's.

Mary Jo wrote me a note as soon as I sat down. She could see I had something tucked under my sweater.

Julie! You found Lihwa!!!!

Yes.

Where was she? Was she in someone's sleeve?

You know.

No, I don't. How would I know where the doll was? What's the matter? You look like

92

you're mad at me or something.

Stop writing me notes. We're supposed to be watching the movie. The doll was in *your* sleeve.

What????!!!! Are you crazy?

I'm not crazy. You are.

No, you are. I didn't take Carolyn's doll!

I found her in your sleeve. You're the only one who has a jacket like that.

But I didn't put her there!

Then who did?

How do I know?

You're the only one I told about the doll. You were there when I took it away from Amy. And you think Lihwa is beautiful.

Yes, but that doesn't mean I stole her. Maybe someone else saw the doll. Maybe someone found that first note I wrote you when I asked if the doll was all right. Maybe someone looked in your desk at lunchtime.

But why did she hide the doll in *your* coat?

I don't know. To make you think it was me? Maybe to make you mad and get me in trouble? If I really hid Lihwa in my coat, why would I tell you it was a good idea to look there? You don't REALLY think I took Carolyn's doll, do you???

94

I don't know.

2:50 p.m.

Dear God,

It's just a few minutes before the bell rings, and kids are cleaning up and putting their papers away.

I have Lihwa back, God, but I feel worse than ever! I could tell I hurt Mary Jo's feelings by not saying I believed her. Sometimes I think the only thing worse than getting your own feelings hurt (like mine were this morning) is when you hurt someone else's feelings. That's because then you feel like a mean person, even if you don't want to be mean.

And now Mary Jo is mad at me because I got mad at her.

But at least I don't have the whole class mad at me. Some kid just asked Miss Mac-

Donald if we would have the puppet show Monday, and she said, "Yes, yes." So anyway, I have the doll back, and I didn't ruin things for the class.

But I'm still not sure about Mary Jo. I mean, I *did* find the doll in her sleeve. And she has done sneaky things before, like hiding the last piece of the jigsaw puzzle.

But, of course, mostly Mary Jo *doesn't* do sneaky things. Mostly you can *count* on her, and she is a good best friend to have.

I don't know.

This has turned out to be a very bad day, God. But at least I got Lihwa back. And now I have one more hard thing to do. I have to run home and put Lihwa back before Carolyn and Amy get home. I hope Amy remembers to walk slow.

Love,
Julie

8:00 p.m.

Dear God,

It is later now—almost Lights Out Time, which comes a little after Bed Time. So I'm writing this in bed. I thought I would just start at the beginning (I mean the beginning after school) and tell you how things turned out—even though you already know. I think it would save a lot of trouble if people knew how things would turn out, but I guess they just don't.

I was so worried about getting Carolyn's doll back in time that as soon as the bell rang, I jumped up, grabbed my jacket, and ran down the hall. You know that I *never* run down the hall, but today I did. Some kids run in the halls all the time, and nothing ever happens. But when *I* ran down the hall, I crashed into a kid who was carrying two big boxes of pebbles for his teacher because she was teaching her kids to do mosaic pictures.

There were pebbles all over the hall—*everywhere*. The kid yelled at me for bumping into him (even though it was an accident), and the kid's teacher said I had no business running down the hall.

I felt like crying, because she probably thought I ran down the hall all the time. It's bad enough to be in trouble with your own teacher, but it's even worse when somebody else's teacher yells at you.

I thought she was going to take me to the principal's office, but she said it was only fair for me to stay and help pick up the pebbles. And she was right, of course, it *was* only fair. But I had a big problem. I had to get Lihwa home before Carolyn got there, and it would take forever to pick up all those pebbles.

That's when Mary Jo came by and asked, "Are you still mad?"

And I said, "No, are you still mad?"

And she said, "No." Then she figured out what had happened with the pebbles. She said that kind of thing happens to her a lot. She said since she could run really fast I should give her Lihwa to take to my house, and she would put her back on the shelf for me and wait for me.

I guess I still sort of wondered how Lihwa got in Mary Jo's sleeve in the first place. But I decided fast that I would just have to give the doll to Mary Jo and hope she took her to my house like she would if she was helping me—and not take it to her house like she would if she was going to steal it.

So we dumped some of the junk out of Mary Jo's book bag and put Lihwa inside.

Then Mary Jo took off, running faster than any kid you ever saw. And I kept picking up pebbles.

What a day.

When I finally got the pebbles picked up, I came out of school—and who did I see ahead of me on the street? *Carolyn and Amy.* I hurried and caught up with them. I figured if things didn't work out with the doll, I'd rather be there when Carolyn found out instead of not be there. That doesn't make sense in a way, but that's how I felt.

Carolyn was yelling at Amy to put on her scarf and mittens, but Amy wasn't obeying very well.

When Carolyn saw me, she said, "Here, you take care of Amy for a while." Then Carolyn went to talk to a friend of hers. And I whispered to Amy, "Don't worry about the doll. Mary Jo is going to get it home for us."

Amy just looked at me and said, "What doll?"

I wanted to scream at her, but I didn't want Carolyn to hear, so I tried to whisper as if I were screaming. "What do you mean, 'What doll,' you little twirp. Lihwa! Carolyn's doll. The one you took this morning for Show and Tell!"

Amy just looked at me again and said, "Oh." Then she said, "Julie, can we make popcorn when we get home?"

Amy can drive a person crazy, God.

I yelled to Carolyn that it was her job to walk Amy home, and then I ran on ahead to see if Mary Jo was waiting for me in my room with the doll safe on the shelf.

She was.

Mary Jo stayed to help me feed Marshmallow, Suki, Sumi, Setsu, and Oreo. And all the time she was helping me, we whispered to each other about who could have played that terrible trick today.

And we agreed that the trick was really against *both* of us—because whoever it was stole from *me* and tried to put the blame on *Mary Jo.*

I told her about what I heard someone say when I went to get my T.A. badge this morning. But we couldn't figure out who it was.

I walked Mary Jo home, and we still talked about it.

Then Mary Jo walked me partway back to my house, and we talked about it some more. But we still couldn't get it all figured out. So we thought of some plans.

Mary Jo and I decided that we would really keep our ears open so that if anyone

103

says to someone else, "By the way, I stole Julie's doll the other day and blamed it on Mary Jo," we'll be right there to jump out and say something like, "Aha! So it was *you!*" Whoever it turns out to be.

We also made a plan to keep our eyes open, so we can watch to see if anyone starts stealing other things. Then we can say, "Did you take Julie's doll, too?"

And another plan we made is to tell Mrs. Whitney when she gets back, but I think we'll wait till after the puppet show. Of course we can't prove anything, and Mrs. Whitney might think the problem is solved already just because we got the doll back.

So those are the plans Mary Jo and I have for school.

But I thought of another plan that I will do just by myself at home. I will ask my mother if I can talk to her in private, and then I'll tell her all about what happened with Carolyn's doll. I will let her decide if I need to tell Carolyn that Lihwa spent the day at school. And I will let her decide if she needs to yell at Amy for taking the doll in the first place. (I already yelled at Amy a little bit, and all she said was, "What doll?" So I'm not sure yelling at her some more will do any good.) But my mother can decide about everything, and I don't have to worry about it. Sometimes not having to decide about something is a load off your mind.

Poor Marshmallow and Oreo! I had to stop writing for a few minutes, God, because they were playing with a balloon Amy left lying around, and the balloon broke. BANG! They didn't understand what happened, and of course it scared them silly.

So I held out my arms, and they came running. And now I am trying to write this with two sweet, little, scared cats on my lap—so you know why my handwriting doesn't look that good anymore.

Of course, Marshmallow and Oreo don't understand what happened. All they know is that I am here to love them and take care of them.

What was I talking about before all that happened? Oh, yes. My plans.

I would like to find out who said that mean thing about me this morning, and I would like to know who took Carolyn's doll. Maybe it was the same person. Maybe it was two people. Maybe I will find out what happened. But you know what I just thought of? Maybe I won't ever find out!

Maybe people can't always understand everything, no matter how much they would like to, right?

Of course, YOU understand everything, God.

And you know what I just thought of? If YOU understand everything, that's a load off my mind.

Good Night, God.

Love,
Julie

If you enjoyed this book in The Kids from Apple Street Church series, you'll want to sneak a look at the diaries of all the kids in Miss Jenkins's Sunday school class.

1. Mary Jo Bennett
2. Danny Petrowski
3. Julie Chang
4. Pug McConnell
5. Becky Garcia*
6. Curtis Anderson*

Available soon

You'll find these books at a Christian bookstore. Or write to Chariot Books, 850 N. Grove, Elgin, IL 60120.